OFFICIAL GUIDE

Paul Sottosanti

SCHOLASTIC INC.

New York   Toronto   London   Auckland   Sydney

Mexico City   New Delhi   Hong Kong   Buenos Aires

ISBN 0-439-66318-0

Published by Scholastic Inc.
SCHOLASTIC and associated logos are trademarks and/or registered trademarks of
Scholastic Inc.

12 11 10 9 8 7 6 5 4 3 2 1   4 5 6 7 8 9/0

Printed in the U.S.A.
First printing, September 2004

WELCOME

In the game of Duel Masters, two duelists summon mythical creatures in the Zone to battle in an intense struggle. Strong duelists such as Shobu Kirifuda are on an endless quest to better themselves so that they can break down the defenses of all challengers.

Study this guide, absorb the concepts, and try out the decks suggested inside. If you haven't played the game before, start with the Basic Gameplay section. If you're already an experienced player, feel free to skip to the Advanced Gameplay section and read up on the strategies that master duelists use.

Remember that practice makes perfect. Engage in as many duels as you can. Sooner than you think, you'll be a master of the duel, just like Shobu!

Own the Zone!

THE WORLD OF DUEL MASTERS

For most players Duel Masters is just a fun game, but elite players actually can bring the card creatures to life. Doing so requires passion and discipline. A martial art, Kaijudo, develops and strengthens this ability. Kaijudo literally means the art of battling with giant monsters.

Large training halls and dueling temples have been built to assist duelists in the art of Kaijudo. In the not so distant past, two men emerged as true Kaijudo champions. One, known only as The Master, had his face scarred in a duel and now runs a temple. The other, Shori Kirifuda, mysteriously disappeared.

the STORY of SHOBU

Shobu Kirifuda, Shori's son, has many fond memories of his dad teaching him to play Duel Masters. Shobu is a good duelist who always does his best but he hasn't yet learned his true potential.

Shobu spends his days like most other kids. His mother makes him clean his room and do his homework, his teacher reminds him not to bring his deck to class, and he duels like all the other kids on the playground. However, his friends Rekuta, Mimi, and Knight know that when it comes to dueling, Shobu has a special talent. He also strives to live by the Kaijudo Code.

The Kaijudo Code

I make no excuses.
My actions are my voice.

I have no enemies.
My opponent is my
teacher.

I need no deceitful tricks.
My character is my sword.

I think not of quitting.
My courage is my secret
weapon.

I know not of defeat.
My experience becomes
my strength.

Kaijudo Duel Terms

The following terms are used while dueling by players who follow the Kaijudo Code:

Kettou da!.......................... I challenge you!
The official request to duel.

Yoshi!....................................I accept!
The formal acceptance of a duel challenge.

Ikuzo!.................................I'm ready!
Said by the first player to have his shield zone set and who is ready for the action to begin.

Koi!.......................................Bring it on!
Said by the first player to have his shield zone set, ready for the action to begin.

Ike!.. Attack!!
Said whenever attacking with a creature. For example, "Bolshack Dragon – ike!!"

Todome da!................The destroying blow!!
Said when all of an opponent's shields are broken, just before the last winning attack.

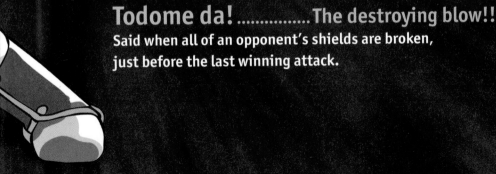

Here are some additional terms that can be used at any time:

Sensei .... Duel Teacher
A duel superior who is a teacher and/or trainer.

Kohai ....Senior Duelist
An older or more experienced duelist.

Senpai...Junior Duelist
A younger or less experienced duelist.

Hai!.........................."Yes!" or "I understand!"
Agreement and confirmation.

Introduction to CIVILIZATIONS

Creatures from all five civilizations inhabit the Zone. Spaceships from the Light civilization, twisted creations from Darkness, tanks from Fire, giant fish from Water, and all manner of plant life from Nature share the same space when a duel is raging.

Master duelists are comfortable with creatures from all five of the civilizations, but there's no shame in specializing in a few of them at first.

Darkness Civilization

Toxic gas and total darkness fill the underground world of the Darkness civilization. Here lifespans are short and inhabitants never stop trying to live forever. Attempts to lengthen their lives have served only to spoil the land.

Experiments have created deadly diseases. Magic-wielding demons command zombies and skeletons. Worms and slimes creep across the landscape consuming anything slow or stupid enough to stay in the way.

Bottom line: You don't want to go there.

Strengths and Weaknesses

The Darkness civilization is strange but flexible. It can go on the offensive with quick creatures backed by spells, or it can set up defenses and then destroy creatures large enough to get through. It's also a good support civilization for decks that need to destroy pesky creatures.

Try out a Darkness deck if you simply like messing with your opponent. There's no better feeling than leaving your opponent empty-handed with no creatures in the battle zone. That's what Darkness does best.

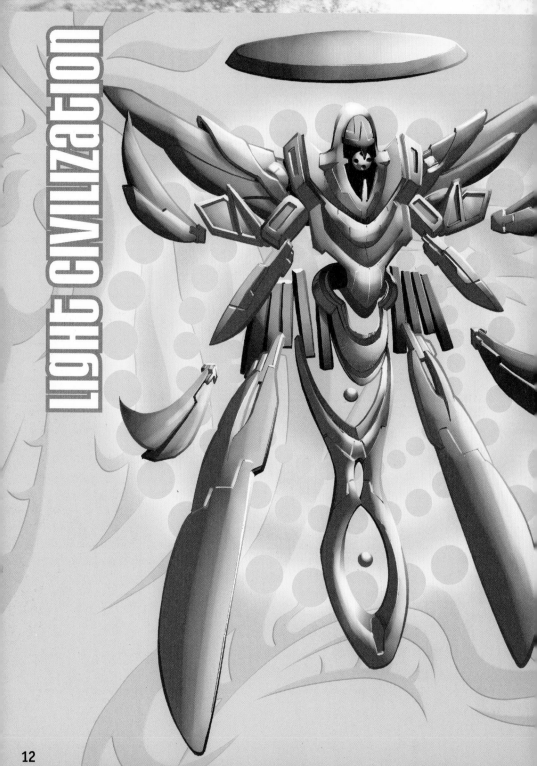

LIGHT

LIGHT CIVILIZATION

The Light world is made up of colonies floating amongst the clouds. Originally, it stayed undisturbed by keeping outsiders out. Their world was the most peaceful place.

Unfortunately, that peace ended when other civilizations lost their homelands and invaded to survive. Light had to fight back with their spaceships and ultra-tech guardians.

Strengths and Weaknesses

Play Light if you like feeling confident and in control, with an army of creatures keeping you safe. But don't think that Light only knows how to defend. With game-changing spells like Diamond Cutter and Holy Awe, victory is never far away.

nature civilization

A jungle covers the largest continent, home to the Nature civilization. In the hot, humid climate, World Trees have grown so tall that they almost touch the cities in the Light world. Their stored energy strengthens the pull of gravity, giving an advantage to Nature creatures used to that effect.

Many races inhabit this unique world, but there are no cities and no one race governs. Instead, might makes right. Even Beast Folk, the most advanced of the races, possess barely any technology.

Strengths and Weaknesses

Play a Nature deck if you think bigger is better! Nature is able to summon huge monsters quickly. Its weakness is a lack of defenses, so take advantage of your creatures' size by engaging in lots of battles. Few duelists will be able to handle the bulk.

Water Civilization

The world of Water is half-land and half-sea. Inhabitants, who once lived only in water, have learned to adapt to the land, too.

Cities are built directly in the water because of the energy resources there. In spite of the depths, the cities are clean and well-lit. At the center is the Tower, shaped like a spiral, where the Cyber Lords float in their tanks. Surrounding the Tower are transparent buildings created from solidified seawater.

Although it's not commonly known, the source of underwater energy is a hidden ocean current. Only a powerful few possess this secret knowledge.

Strengths and Weaknesses

The Water civilization is very tricky. It can use many different strategies, depending on what will be most effective. Try out Water if you value flexibility over raw power and want to win with brains and not brawn.

Fire Civilization

The arid Fire civilization stretches over islands covered in volcanic ash and hardened lava, shaken by constant earthquakes and volcanic eruptions. Very little plant life survives.

Volcanoes are the symbol of power. Dragonoids have learned how to trigger an eruption and use it as a weapon. Although it requires months of preparation, and aiming is difficult, this volcano weapon is overwhelmingly destructive.

Fire creatures make their own gunpowder and mine for iron. Once a mountain has been hollowed, they transform it into a fortress reinforced with metal. They build steam engines for transportation, and use the smoke clouds as shields.

Strengths and Weaknesses

Fire is all about aggression and chaos. Try the Fire civilization if you like to go all out, risking everything in a reckless assault on your opponent's shields. Attacking every turn is almost a necessity. Win or lose, your duels will end quickly. The quicker, the better.

Choosing a Deck

Decks need to be a minimum of forty cards, with no more than four copies of any single card. Other than that, you can build a deck any way you want. Shuffle almost any pile of cards and you'll still be able to summon creatures and cast spells.

Some cards are better than others, though, and some cards work together especially well. Once you've gotten booster packs, check out the Deck Building section for detailed strategy tips.

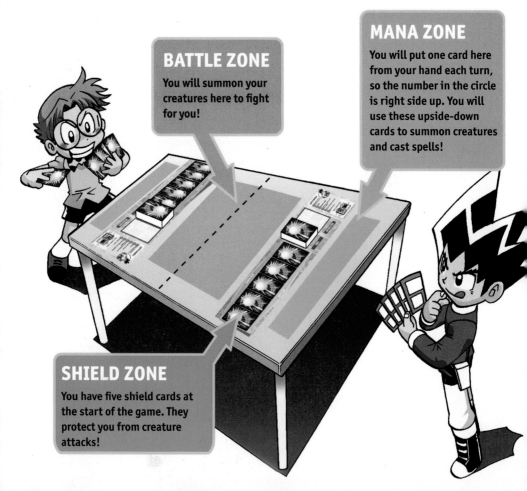

MANA ZONE
You will put one card here from your hand each turn, so the number in the circle is right side up. You will use these upside-down cards to summon creatures and cast spells!

BATTLE ZONE
You will summon your creatures here to fight for you!

SHIELD ZONE
You have five shield cards at the start of the game. They protect you from creature attacks!

Preparing for a Duel

First, shuffle your deck a few times so the order of the cards is random. Then take the top five cards — without looking at them — and lay them facedown in a line in front of you. These are your shields.

Next, take five more cards from your deck and look at them. This is your hand, where you keep all the spells you haven't yet cast and the creatures you haven't yet summoned.

Flip a coin to see if you or your opponent goes first. After that, you will take turns until someone has won the duel.

How do you win?

Attack with your creatures to knock out all of your opponent's shields . . . and then attack one last time.

Taking Your Turn

Follow these steps:

1 Straighten out any of your cards that were turned sideways on your last turn. Turning cards sideways is called tapping and straightening them is called untapping. You'll learn why to tap cards in step four.

Untap the cards in your mana zone by turning them upside down so you can read their mana numbers.

2 If you're going first and it's your very first turn of the duel, skip this step. Otherwise, take the top card of your deck and add it to your hand of cards.

Drawing a card.

Choose a card from your hand and put it upside down in your mana zone so that you're looking at the circled white number at the bottom. If you already have a lot of cards in your mana zone and not many in your hand, skip this step.

Putting a card into your mana zone

Now you can summon your creatures! The number in a creature card's top left corner is the amount of mana you need to summon it. Tap (turn sideways) a number of cards in your mana zone equal to that number. At least one of the cards that you tap must be of the same civilization as the creature. Once you've tapped enough mana, place the creature (untapped) into the battle zone.

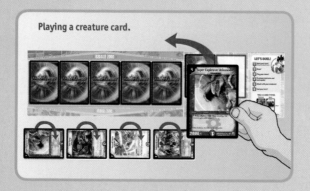

Playing a creature card.

You can also cast any spells that are in your hand. These work just like creatures except that you don't put them in the battle zone. Simply tap the mana, do whatever the spell says, and put it in your graveyard.

It's time to attack! Creatures that you summoned this turn have "summoning sickness" and can't attack yet. Attack with creatures that were in the battle zone at the start of your turn. Tap the creature and announce that it's attacking. You can attack with as many or as few creatures as you want, but finish each attack before starting the next.

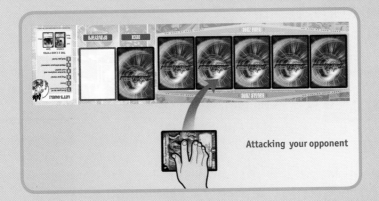

Attacking your opponent

Creatures can either attack your opponent or attack one of his tapped creatures. Untapped creatures can't be attacked. If you attack your opponent, you'll break one of his shields. He picks it up from his shield zone and puts it in his hand. If he has no shields left and you attack him, you've won!

If you attack a tapped creature, the two creatures will battle.

A battle is simply comparing the power numbers of the two creatures. The creature with the lowest power goes to the graveyard. If there's a tie, they both go to the graveyard.

That's it! You're done with your turn, and now your opponent runs through the same five steps. Then it's your turn again.

There are three ways to easily recognize a creature card:

- The art is in a rectangular shape
- There's a number in the bottom left corner representing the creature's power
- The creature has a race (i.e. Beast Folk) written under its name

Some creatures also have special abilities listed on the card. For example:

Power Attacker

A Fire or Nature creature with Power Attacker +2000 gets to add 2000 points to its power in the middle of an attack. This lets you win battles against much bigger creatures than you otherwise could. This ability is also marked on the card with a "+" after the power number.

Blocker

Some creatures from the Light, Water, or Darkness civilizations have a little blue Blocker icon. Whenever your opponent declares that he is attacking, you have the option of tapping one of your Blocker creatures. Then the attacker and the Blocker creature battle. Even if your Blocker loses, you won't lose a shield.

Slayer

Usually only Darkness creatures have this ability. When a Slayer creature battles, its opponent is doomed. If the Slayer loses, both creatures die. If it wins, only the enemy dies. Even tiny creatures can be very useful if they are Slayers.

Double Breaker

Double Breakers break two shields when they attack! If your opponent only has one shield left, only that shield is broken — you still have to attack once more to win the game. This ability is reserved for the largest and meanest creatures in the Zone.

Evolution Creature

Added in Evo-Crushinators of Doom, evolution creatures are the evolved forms of the monsters under your command. The cards are placed on top of a creature of the proper race in the battle zone. The two cards are now the same creature. If the creature is destroyed, both cards go to the graveyard. If a spell sends it into your hand, both cards go into your hand. Not only are evolution creatures the biggest, baddest, and meanest creatures around, but they can attack the turn you summon them, too. Many are even Double Breakers!

Spell Abilities

Spell cards have their art within an arched shape and don't have a power number. They can only be used once and then go to the graveyard. Spells can be extremely useful: destroying enemy creatures, making your creatures unblockable, or searching your deck for the exact creature you need, for example.

Spells can also have Shield Triggers.

Shield Trigger

Look for a little icon of a lightning bolt inside of a black diamond.

When an opponent breaks one of your shields and it has this icon, play the spell right away. You don't even have to tap any cards in your mana zone! These cards give you a chance to come from behind and punish your opponent for breaking your shields.

Putting Cards in Your Mana Zone

In Duel Masters, you have to start making important decisions right away. On the first turn, you'll have a full hand of cards and one of them needs to be placed in the mana zone. This may seem a little overwhelming, but keep the following ideas in mind:

Put creatures and spells that cost a lot of mana into the mana zone early. A creature that costs six mana, like Bolshack Dragon, can't be summoned until at least your sixth turn. Keep creatures that cost less mana in your hand early on so you can summon them sooner. Later you can play larger creatures when you draw them. Of course, if you have a creature that's very strong against your opponent, like Scarlet Skyterror against a deck filled with Blockers, hold it in your hand until you can cast it.

Shield Trigger spells often cost a lot of mana. They're best in your shield zone or in your mana zone, not in your hand.

To cast a card from your hand, you need to have a card of the same civilization in your mana zone. Make sure to place a card from each of your civilizations into the mana zone as early as possible.

Learn when to stop putting cards in your mana zone. This depends on the mana ceiling of your deck — the cost of the most expensive cards that you want to cast. If you don't have any creatures that cost more than six mana, for example, then don't put a seventh card into your mana zone. Instead, hold the extra creature in your hand to summon it.

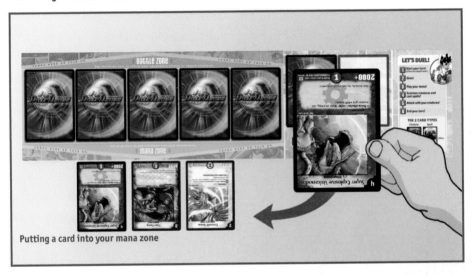

Putting a card into your mana zone

Exception #1: When you have a lot of cards in your hand — maybe because your shields are getting broken and you need to catch up — go ahead and put cards in the mana zone so that you can summon creatures quickly and regain the advantage.

Exception #2: When you draw a spell that's useless against your opponent — like Critical Blade against a Fire/Nature deck — put it in the mana zone to get some use out of it.

KEEP CREATURES THAT COST LESS MANA IN YOUR HAND EARLY ON SO THAT YOU CAN SUMMON THEM IN THE EARLY TURNS.

Breaking Your Opponent's Shields

To win, you need to get one creature through your opponent's defenses. This is a lot harder than it sounds, because your opponent will be casting spells and summoning creatures, too, and five shields stand between you and victory. So, every opportunity you get to break a shield, you should take it — right?

It's not that simple. When you break a shield, you're risking getting hit by a Shield Trigger, and you're also giving your opponent a new card to use. That's fine if you're playing a fast game and plan to win before the broken shields matter. Otherwise, remember that each shield you break could return as a new creature confronting you.

Pay attention when your opponent starts breaking your shields early. The extra cards in your hand can be put in the mana zone to always have creatures to summon. But the same thing's true for your opponent!

As a general rule, only attack your opponent directly when you can defeat him in the next few turns. The sooner you win after your initial attack, the less time he has to use the extra cards to turn the game around. Although it sounds crazy, sometimes you should end your turn without attacking even if you have the only creature on the board.

The Combat Phase

Although attacking shields can be dangerous, attacking tapped creatures is almost always a good idea. Each time you destroy a creature without losing one of your own, you're gaining a small advantage.

Remember that each Blocker intercepts only one attack. Then they're tapped and vulnerable. Attack with your smaller creatures first, so that if your opponent uses a Blocker to destroy your creature, you can then smash his Blocker with a larger creature.

Or attack with creatures larger than the Blocker. Your opponent still can intercept the attack, but the Blocker will die and you won't lose anything.

Don't forget that your attacking creatures will be tapped on your opponent's turn. Only attack when you can destroy more of his creatures than you're going to lose yourself except when you're low on shields and need to destroy his creatures to stay alive.

Knowing when to attack is one of the keys of becoming a successful Duel Master.

BUILD UP ENOUGH SMALL ADVANTAGES AND YOU'LL OWN THE BATTLE ZONE!

cards

The following pages contain pictures of the cards from the Duel Masters Base Set and the first two expansions sets, Evo-Crushinators of Doom and Rampage of the Super Warriors.

The Base Set contains 120 different cards:

- ✚ 10 super rare
- ✪ 10 very rare
- ★ 30 rare
- ✦ 30 uncommon
- ● 40 common

The two expansion sets each contain 60 cards:

- ✚ 5 super rare
- ✪ 5 very rare
- ★ 15 rare
- ✦ 15 uncommon
- ● 20 common

Each expansion set contains creatures and spells that can make your deck better. If you have a lot of cards from the base set, start getting cards from Evo-Crushinators of Doom and Rampage of the Super Warriors. The best duelists use the most effective cards from each of the sets.

LIGHT

Hanusa, Radiance Elemental
7 — ANGEL COMMAND

- Double breaker (This creature breaks 2 shields.)

The sky was scorched by Dragons' fire, and the earth gouged by elementals' rays. The battle raged for seven nights and seven days.

9500 — 51/110

Urth, Purifying Elemental
6 — ANGEL COMMAND

- Double breaker (This creature breaks 2 shields.)
- At the end of each of your turns, you may untap this creature.

It is said the destruction of the Ancient Empire was caused by the descent of the elemental gods.

6000 — 50/110

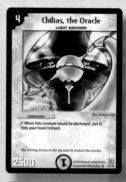

Chilias, the Oracle
4 — LIGHT BRINGER

- When this creature would be destroyed, put it into your hand instead.

The shining towers in the sky exist to protect the oracles.

2500 — 1/110

Dia Nork, Moonlight Guardian
4 — GUARDIAN

- Blocker (When an opponent's creature attacks, you may tap this creature to stop the attack. Then the two creatures battle.)
- This creature can't attack players.

Flying is the greatest taboo of any race that has encountered the Guardians.

5000 — 3/110

Emerald Grass
2 — STARLIGHT TREE

- Blocker (When an opponent's creature attacks, you may tap this creature to stop the attack. Then the two creatures battle.)
- This creature can't attack players.

3000 — 5/110

Frei, Vizier of Air
4 — INITIATE

- At the end of each of your turns, you may untap this creature.

"Vizier of Air, arise. Your fingers are sacred swords."
—Hanusa, Radiance Elemental

3000 — 4/110

Gran Gure, Space Guardian
6 — GUARDIAN

- Blocker (When an opponent's creature attacks, you may tap this creature to stop the attack. Then the two creatures battle.)
- This creature can't attack players.

Those who defile the Sky Castle are doomed, for they shall know the wrath of the Guardians.

9000 — 3/110

Holy Awe
6 — SPELL

- Shield trigger (When this spell is put into your hand from your shield zone, you may cast it immediately for no cost.)
- Tap all your opponent's creatures in the battle zone.

6/110

Iere, Vizier of Bullets
3 — INITIATE

"Vizier of Bullets, arise. Your will is an arrow that never misses the target." —Hanusa, Radiance Elemental

3000 — 5/110

Iocant, the Oracle
2 — LIGHT BRINGER

- Blocker (When an opponent's creature attacks, you may tap this creature to stop the attack. Then the two creatures battle.)
- While you have at least 1 Angel Command in the battle zone, this creature gets +2000 power.
- This creature can't attack players.

2000+ — 6/110

La Ura Giga, Sky Guardian
1 — GUARDIAN

- Blocker (When an opponent's creature attacks, you may tap this creature to stop the attack. Then the two creatures battle.)
- This creature can't attack players.

To protect their floating cities, Guardians are gifted with shining wings.

2000 — 9/110

Lah, Purification Enforcer
5 — BERSERKER

Those who have seen this Enforcer believe that eclipses are omens of disaster.

5500 — 10/110

Laser Wing

5

SPELL

- Choose up to 2 of your creatures in the battle zone. They can't be blocked this turn.

This is light speed.

©2004 Wizards of the Coast/
Shogakukan/Mitsui-Kids 11/110

Lok, Vizier of Hunting

4

INITIATE

CREATURE

"Vizier of Hunting, arise. Your words are arrows of light."
—Hanusa, Radiance Elemental

4000

©2004 Wizards of the Coast/
Shogakukan/Mitsui-Kids 12/110

Miele, Vizier of Lightning

3

INITIATE

CREATURE

- When you put this creature into the battle zone, you may choose 1 of your opponent's creatures in the battle zone and tap it.

"Vizier of Lightning, arise. Your eyes are a bow of judgment."
—Hanusa, Radiance Elemental

1000

©2004 Wizards of the Coast/
Shogakukan/Mitsui-Kids 13/110

Moonlight Flash

4

SPELL

- Choose up to 2 of your opponent's creatures in the battle zone and tap them.

Cower before the purity of the Angel Commands!

©2004 Wizards of the Coast/
Shogakukan/Mitsui-Kids 14/110

Rayla, Truth Enforcer

6

BERSERKER

CREATURE

- When you put this creature into the battle zone, search your deck. You may take a spell from your deck, show that spell to your opponent, and put it into your hand. Then shuffle your deck.

The Enforcers deliver the oracles' words, which bear the power of truth.

3000

©2004 Wizards of the Coast/
Shogakukan/Mitsui-Kids 15/110

Reusol, the Oracle

2

LIGHT BRINGER

CREATURE

Soul and light enmeshed in a web of glory.

2000

©2004 Wizards of the Coast/
Shogakukan/Mitsui-Kids 16/110

Ruby Grass

3

STARLIGHT TREE

CREATURE

- Blocker *(When an opponent's creature attacks, you may tap this creature to stop the attack. Then the two creatures battle.)*
- This creature can't attack players.
- At the end of each of your turns, you may untap this creature.

3000

©2004 Wizards of the Coast/
Shogakukan/Mitsui-Kids 17/110

Senatine Jade Tree

3

STARLIGHT TREE

CREATURE

- Blocker *(When an opponent's creature attacks, you may tap this creature to stop the attack. Then the two creatures battle.)*
- This creature can't attack players.

Floating trees in the sky generate beautiful light from poisoned air.

4000

©2004 Wizards of the Coast/
Shogakukan/Mitsui-Kids 18/110

Solar Ray

2

SPELL

- Shield trigger *(When this spell is put into your hand from your shield zone, you may cast it immediately for no cost.)*
- Choose 1 of your opponent's creatures in the battle zone and tap it.

©2004 Wizards of the Coast/
Shogakukan/Mitsui-Kids 19/110

Sonic Wing

3

SPELL

- Choose 1 of your creatures in the battle zone. It can't be blocked this turn.

"Can't catch me!"

©2004 Wizards of the Coast/
Shogakukan/Mitsui-Kids 20/110

Szubs Kin, Twilight Guardian

5

GUARDIAN

CREATURE

- Blocker *(When an opponent's creature attacks, you may tap this creature to stop the attack. Then the two creatures battle.)*
- This creature can't attack players.

Those who dwell in the sky towers eradicate all intruders.

6000

©2004 Wizards of the Coast/
Shogakukan/Mitsui-Kids 21/110

Toel, Vizier of Hope

5

INITIATE

CREATURE

- At the end of each of your turns, you may untap all your creatures in the battle zone.

"Vizier of Hope, arise. Your singing voice is a breeze of dawn."
—Hanusa, Radiance Elemental

2000

©2004 Wizards of the Coast/
Shogakukan/Mitsui-Kids 22/110

water

Aqua Sniper
8 — LIQUID PEOPLE

CREATURE

• When you put this creature into the battle zone, choose up to 2 creatures in the battle zone and return them to their owners' hands.

Water surrounds, enfolds, buoys . . . and attacks.

5000

King Depthcon
7 — LEVIATHAN

CREATURE

• Double breaker (This creature breaks 2 shields.)
• This creature can't be blocked.

Leviathans are just like storms. All you can do is wait until they pass.

6000

Aqua Hulcus
3 — LIQUID PEOPLE

CREATURE

• When you put this creature into the battle zone, you may draw a card.

Liquid People freely control Dipold. For them, water is armor and shield.

2000

Aqua Knight
5 — LIQUID PEOPLE

CREATURE

• When this creature would be destroyed, return it to your hand instead.

Like a whirlpool, it never seems to end.

4000

Aqua Soldier
3 — LIQUID PEOPLE

CREATURE

• When this creature would be destroyed, return it to your hand instead.

"What a spirit for such a skinny little thing." —Brawler Zyler

1000

Aqua Vehicle
2 — LIQUID PEOPLE

CREATURE

The chip implanted in its head lets the Cyber Lords control its brain waves.

1000

Brain Serum
4

SPELL

• Shield trigger (When this spell is put into your hand from your shield zone, you may cast it immediately for no cost.)
• Draw up to 2 cards.

Candy Drop
3 — CYBER VIRUS

CREATURE

• This creature can't be blocked.

No mouth. Big bite.

1000

Crystal Memory
4

SPELL

• Shield trigger (When this spell is put into your hand from your shield zone, you may cast it immediately for no cost.)
• Search your deck. You may take a card from your deck and put it into your hand. Then shuffle your deck.

Faerie Child
4 — CYBER VIRUS

CREATURE

• This creature can't be blocked.

A school of teeny, tiny points of light. Stopping them all is impossible.

2000

Hunter Fish
2 — FISH

CREATURE

• Blocker (When an opponent's creature attacks, you may tap this creature to stop the attack. Then the two creatures battle.)
• This creature can't attack.

It lies in wait, hidden in coral reefs, lashing out ferociously when it senses prey.

3000

Illusionary Merfolk
5 — GEL FISH

CREATURE

• When you put this creature into the battle zone, if you have a Cyber Lord in the battle zone, draw a card.

The Cyber Lords' devotion to beauty is so extreme, they even designed their warrior race to have a pleasant appearance.

4000

King Coral
LEVIATHAN

3

Illus. Hideaki Takamura

CREATURE

🛡 Blocker (When an opponent's creature attacks, you may tap this creature to stop the attack. Then the two creatures battle.)

Leviathans mature slowly, eventually growing to become the largest creatures in the world.

1000

King Ripped-Hide
LEVIATHAN

7

Illus. Mike Masterharran

CREATURE

• When you put this creature into the battle zone, draw up to 2 cards.

Long ago, the Cyber Lords built a city on his back.

5000

Marine Flower
CYBER VIRUS

1

Illus. Hikaru Iwano

CREATURE

🛡 Blocker (When an opponent's creature attacks, you may tap this creature to stop the attack. Then the two creatures battle.)
• This creature can't attack.

It blooms in the ocean depths, far from any light.

2000

Phantom Fish
GEL FISH

3

Illus. Ittoku

CREATURE

🛡 Blocker (When an opponent's creature attacks, you may tap this creature to stop the attack. Then the two creatures battle.)
• This creature can't attack.

4000

Revolver Fish
GEL FISH

4

Illus. Naoki Saito

CREATURE

🛡 Blocker (When an opponent's creature attacks, you may tap this creature to stop the attack. Then the two creatures battle.)
• This creature can't attack.

5000

Saucer-Head Shark
GEL FISH

5

Illus. Naoki Saito

CREATURE

• When you put this creature into the battle zone, return each creature in the battle zone that has power 2000 or less to its owner's hand.

"Isn't it cool? The heads can be combined." —Tropico

3000

Seamine
FISH

6

Illus. Tomohumi Ogasawara

CREATURE

🛡 Blocker (When an opponent's creature attacks, you may tap this creature to stop the attack. Then the two creatures battle.)

If the last thing in your life you want to see is something beautiful, attack an underwater city.

4000

Spiral Gate
2

Illus. Toshihiro Ogasawara

SPELL

🛡 Shield trigger (When this spell is put into your hand from your shield zone, you may cast it immediately for no cost.)
• Choose 1 creature in the battle zone and return it to its owner's hand.

Teleportation
5

Illus. Akihane Yamamoto

SPELL

• Choose up to 2 creatures in the battle zone and return them to their owners' hands.

"Start all over from your previous life!" —Crystal Lancer

Tropico
CYBER LORD

5

Illus. Jason

CREATURE

• This creature can't be blocked while you have at least 2 other creatures in the battle zone.

"I will lead you into battle."

3000

Unicorn Fish
FISH

4

Illus. Masako Kumatani

CREATURE

• When you put this creature into the battle zone, you may choose 1 creature in the battle zone and return it to its owner's hand.

It attacks anything that enters its territory, even Leviathans.

1000

Virtual Tripwire
3

Illus. Akihane Yamamoto

SPELL

• Choose 1 of your opponent's creatures in the battle zone and tap it.

It will stay until it dies.

Base set

Darkness

7 · Deathliger, Lion of Chaos
DEMON COMMAND

CREATURE

- Double breaker *(This creature breaks 2 shields.)*

The world is deafened by the roar of the deathliger.

9000

---

6 · Zagaan, Knight of Darkness
DEMON COMMAND

CREATURE

- Double breaker *(This creature breaks 2 shields.)*

"If I were to send him to the field, he would overwhelm the enemy in an instant. Where is the fun in that?"
— Ballom, Master of Death

7000

---

1 · Black Feather, Shadow of Rage
GHOST

CREATURE

- When you put this creature into the battle zone, destroy 1 of your creatures.

3000

---

2 · Bloody Squito
BRAIN JACKER

CREATURE

- Blocker *(When an opponent's creature attacks, you may tap this creature to stop the attack. Then the two creatures battle.)*
- This creature can't attack.
- When this creature wins a battle, destroy it.

4000

---

4 · Bone Assassin, the Ripper
LIVING DEAD

CREATURE

- Slayer *(When this creature loses a battle, destroy the other creature.)*

Commanders send them to the front line. It's too dangerous to have them close.

2000

---

3 · Bone Spider
LIVING DEAD

CREATURE

- When this creature wins a battle, destroy it.

They can wait forever, for they know they will not die alone.

5000

---

1 · Creeping Plague

SPELL

- Whenever any of your creatures becomes blocked this turn, it gets "slayer" until the end of the turn. *(When a creature that has "slayer" loses a battle, destroy the other creature.)*

Witness the power of the Dark!

---

4 · Dark Clown
BRAIN JACKER

CREATURE

- Blocker *(When an opponent's creature attacks, you may tap this creature to stop the attack. Then the two creatures battle.)*
- This creature can't attack.
- When this creature wins a battle, destroy it.

6000

---

4 · Dark Raven, Shadow of Grief
GHOST

CREATURE

- Blocker *(When an opponent's creature attacks, you may tap this creature to stop the attack. Then the two creatures battle.)*

If you've ever thought there was something hiding in the dark, you were right.

1000

---

2 · Dark Reversal

SPELL

- Shield trigger *(When this spell is put into your hand from your shield zone, you may cast it immediately for no cost.)*
- Return a creature from your graveyard to your hand.

---

4 · Death Smoke

SPELL

- Destroy 1 of your opponent's untapped creatures.

Savor the taste of fear!

---

2 · Ghost Touch

SPELL

- Shield trigger *(When this spell is put into your hand from your shield zone, you may cast it immediately for no cost.)*
- Your opponent discards a card at random from his hand.

Gigaberos
5 — CHIMERA

- When you put this creature into the battle zone, destroy 2 of your other creatures or destroy this creature.
- Double breaker (This creature breaks 2 shields.)

By assembling parts of different magical beasts, the Dark Lords created a nightmare.

8000

Gigagiele
5 — CHIMERA

- Slayer (When this creature loses a battle, destroy the other creature.)

By assembling parts of different magical beasts, the Dark Lords created a nightmare.

3000

Gigargon
8 — CHIMERA

- When you put this creature into the battle zone, return up to 2 creatures from your graveyard to your hand.

There is no rest in the Dark Realm, even after death.

3000

Masked Horror, Shadow of Scorn
5 — GHOST

- When you put this creature into the battle zone, your opponent discards a card at random from his hand.

Seeking to live forever, they left their bodies behind.

1000

Night Master, Shadow of Decay
6 — GHOST

- Blocker (When an opponent's creature attacks, you may tap this creature to stop the attack. Then the two creatures battle.)

Don't turn around. You wouldn't want to see what's behind you.

3000

Skeleton Soldier, the Defiled
4 — LIVING DEAD

"Rip. Tear. Gnash. They all make the same delightful noises."

3000

Stinger Worm
3 — PARASITE WORM

- When you put this creature into the battle zone, destroy 1 of your creatures.

When worms kill a creature, they can still make it move.

5000

Swamp Worm
7 — PARASITE WORM

- When you put this creature into the battle zone, your opponent chooses 1 of his creatures and destroys it.

Flesh is its food. Bones are its toothpicks.

2000

Terror Pit
6 — SPELL

- Shield trigger (When this spell is put into your hand from your shield zone, you may cast it immediately for no cost.)
- Destroy 1 of your opponent's creatures.

Vampire Silphy
8 — DARK LORD

- When you put this creature into the battle zone, destroy all creatures that have power 3000 or less.

Dark Lords have no mercy for the weak.

4000

Wandering Braineater
2 — LIVING DEAD

- Blocker (When an opponent's creature attacks, you may tap this creature to stop the attack. Then the two creatures battle.)
- This creature can't attack.

Devouring mice, fresh brains is all they know . . . and all they care about.

2000

Writhing Bone Ghoul
2 — LIVING DEAD

Seeking power, they gave up their intelligence. What they found was pain.

2000

Astrocomet Dragon
7 — ARMORED DRAGON

CREATURE
- Power attacker +4000 (While attacking, this creature gets +4000 power.)
- Double breaker (This creature breaks 2 shields.)

Even the smallest wizard attains that has enough firepower to lay waste to a billion.

6000+

Scarlet Skyterror
8 — ARMORED WYVERN

CREATURE
- When you put this creature into the battle zone, destroy all creatures that have "blocker."

The forces of Fire will be mobilized.

3000

Armored Walker Urherion
4 — ARMORLOID

CREATURE
- While you have at least 1 Human in the battle zone, this creature gets +2000 power during its attacks.

"The world at peace? I'd rather see the world in pieces."

3000+

Artisan Picora
1 — MACHINE EATER

CREATURE
- When you put this creature into the battle zone, put 1 card from your mana zone into your graveyard.

"Fix it? That's easy. Just let it." —Legendary Artisan Picora

2000

Bolshack Dragon
6 — ARMORED DRAGON

CREATURE
- While attacking, this creature gets +1000 power for each fire card in your graveyard.
- Double breaker (This creature breaks 2 shields.)

The last city that offended it is now a ruin.

6000+

Brawler Zyler
2 — HUMAN

CREATURE
- Power attacker +2000 (While attacking, this creature gets +2000 power.)

"I wouldn't, if I were you. You don't want to get hurt."

1000+

Burning Power
1

SPELL
- One of your creatures gets "power attacker +2000" until the end of the turn. (While attacking, a creature that has "power attacker +2000" gets +2000 power.)

Witness the power of whirling fire!

Chaos Strike
2

SPELL
- Choose 1 of your opponent's untapped creatures in the battle zone. Your creatures can attack it this turn as though it were tapped.

"You won't escape me!"

Crimson Hammer
2

SPELL
- Destroy 1 of your opponent's creatures that has power 2000 or less.

There's nothing a Machine Eater enjoys more than a good game of Whack-a-Hulcus.

Deadly Fighter Braid Claw
1 — DRAGONOID

CREATURE
- This creature attacks each turn if able.

A Dragonoid's true home is the battlefield.

1000

Draglide
5 — ARMORED WYVERN

CREATURE
- This creature attacks each turn if able.

Draglides grow with their mounts. Their bond is their weapon.

5000

Explosive Fighter Ucarn
5 — DRAGONOID

CREATURE
- When you put this creature into the battle zone, put 2 cards from your mana zone into your graveyard.
- Double breaker (This creature breaks 2 shields.)

Dragonoid fighters never retreat. They believe that a heroic fighter will become a Dragon in his next life.

9000

Fatal Attacker Horvath
3 | HUMAN

- While you have at least 1 Armorloid in the battle zone, this creature gets +2000 power during its attacks.

"Any final words?"

2000+

Fire Sweeper Burning Hellion
4 | DRAGONOID

- Power attacker +2000 (While attacking, this creature gets +2000 power.)

Those who leave battle last are the ones who savor victory the longest.

3000+

Gatling Skyterror
7 | ARMORED WYVERN

- This creature can attack untapped creatures.
- Double breaker (This creature breaks 2 shields.)

Part chopper, part chomper.

7000

Immortal Baron, Vorg
2 | HUMAN

"You see? The one who wins is the one who has the bigger weapon."

2000

Magma Gazer
3

- One of your creatures gets "power attacker +4000" and "double breaker" until the end of the turn. (A creature that has "power attacker +4000" and "double breaker" gets +4000 power while attacking and breaks 2 shields.)

Meteosaur
5 | ROCK BEAST

- When you put this creature into the battle zone, you may destroy 1 of your opponent's creatures that has power 2000 or less.

2000

Nomad Hero Gigio
5 | MACHINE EATER

- This creature can attack untapped creatures.

"Time to move on. So many unexplored worlds, so much trash to find!" —Nomad Hero Gigio

3000

Onslaughter Triceps
3 | DRAGONOID

- When you put this creature into the battle zone, put 1 card from your mana zone into your graveyard.

The first to the front lines are the first to taste victory.

5000

Rothus, the Traveler
4 | ARMORLOID

- When you put this creature into the battle zone, destroy 1 of your creatures. Then your opponent chooses 1 of his creatures and destroys it.

"Though battered and scarred, I march on through wars, storms, and strife. I march on."

4000

Stonesaur
5 | ROCK BEAST

- Power attacker +2000 (While attacking, this creature gets +2000 power.)

There is no sanctuary in the Fire Territory. Especially on the featureless, rocky plains.

4000+

Super Explosive Volcanodon
4 | DRAGONOID

- Power attacker +4000 (While attacking, this creature gets +4000 power.)

After it attacks, the lucky ones are left with rubble.

2000+

Tornado Flame
5

- Shield trigger (When this spell is put into your hand from your shield zone, you may cast it immediately for no cost.)
- Destroy 1 of your opponent's creatures that has power 4000 or less.

Base Set

nature

5 · Deathblade Beetle
GIANT INSECT

CREATURE

- Power attacker +4000 (While attacking, this creature gets +4000 power.)
- Double breaker (This creature breaks 2 shields.)

It devours all...

3000+

7 · Roaring Great-Horn
HORNED BEAST

CREATURE

- Power attacker +2000 (While attacking, this creature gets +2000 power.)
- Double breaker (This creature breaks 2 shields.)

With a mighty cry and mighty roar, the Horned Beasts arose.

8000+

4 · Aura Blast

- Each of your creatures in the battle zone gets "power attacker +2000" until the end of the turn. (While attacking, a creature that has "power attacker +2000" gets +2000 power.)

Hear the roar of the mighty Earth!

3 · Bronze-Arm Tribe
BEAST FOLK

CREATURE

- When you put this creature into the battle zone, put the top card of your deck into your mana zone.

They're bringing some friends to the party.

1000

2 · Burning Mane
BEAST FOLK

CREATURE

It pulled a young tree up by the roots, swinging it over its head as though it were a twig.

2000

4 · Coiling Vines
TREE FOLK

CREATURE

- When this creature would be destroyed, put it into your mana zone instead.

They eat vegetarians.

3000

3 · Dimension Gate

SPELL

- ⚡ Shield trigger (When this spell is put into your hand from your shield zone, you may cast it immediately for no cost.)
- Search your deck. You may take a creature from your deck, show that creature to your opponent, and put it into your hand. Then shuffle your deck.

4 · Dome Shell
COLONY BEETLE

CREATURE

- Power attacker +2000 (While attacking, this creature gets +2000 power.)

Colony Beetles feed on the World Tree to build gigantic nests on their backs.

3000+

3 · Fear Fang
BEAST FOLK

CREATURE

The Beast Folk are gifted with huge muscles to withstand the tremendous gravity of the World Tree.

3000

4 · Forest Hornet
GIANT INSECT

CREATURE

With its deadly sting and crushing jaws, it makes the Horned Beasts cower.

4000

3 · Golden Wing Striker
BEAST FOLK

CREATURE

- Power attacker +2000 (While attacking, this creature gets +2000 power.)

Hawk warriors hurl themselves faster than the wind.

2000+

3 · Mighty Shouter
BEAST FOLK

CREATURE

- When this creature would be destroyed, put it into your mana zone instead.

"I am not pink!"

2000

Natural Snare
6

- **Shield trigger** (When this spell is put into your hand from your shield zone, you may cast it immediately for no cost.)
- Choose 1 of your opponent's creatures in the battle zone and put it into his mana zone.

Pangaea's Song
1

- Put 1 of your creatures from the battle zone into your mana zone.

"Here's something better for you to do."—Fighter Duel Fang

Poisonous Dahlia
4
TREE FOLK

- This creature can't attack players.

"I will never give you up."—Symbolic meaning of the poisonous dahlia in flower language

5000

Poisonous Mushroom
2
BALLOON MUSHROOM

- When you put this creature into the battle zone, you may put 1 card from your hand into your mana zone.

You won't find these mushrooms on salads.

1000

Red-Eye Scorpion
5
GIANT INSECT

- When this creature would be destroyed, put it into your mana zone instead.

Never start a fire in the depths of a forest. Enraged red-eye scorpions will come after you.

4000

Stampeding Longhorn
5
HORNED BEAST

- This creature can't be blocked by any creature that has power 3000 or less.

A stampeding longhorn leaves nothing but dust in its wake.

4000

Steel Smasher
2
BEAST FOLK

- This creature can't attack players.

"Me big. Me tough. Me smash." —Dan Hammer, Beast Warrior

3000

Storm Shell
7
COLONY BEETLE

- When you put this creature into the battle zone, your opponent chooses 1 of his creatures in the battle zone and puts it into his mana zone.

A Colony Beetle's spawning is a virtual nightmare. It covers the earth with a hell of its bullet-like eggs.

2000

Thorny Mandra
5
TREE FOLK

- When you put this creature into the battle zone, you may put 1 creature from your graveyard into your mana zone.

A beautiful flower, an alluring scent . . . and deadly thorns.

4000

Tower Shell
6
COLONY BEETLE

- This creature can't be blocked by any creature that has power 4000 or less.

Not many things want to get in its way.

5000

Tri-horn Shepherd
5
HORNED BEAST

Sometimes weeks pass before it realizes it has a gored enemy stuck to its horns.

5000

Ultimate Force
5

- Put the top 2 cards of your deck into your mana zone.

"Great Earth, give me your might!" —Fighter Duel Fang

super-rares

6 Ladia Bale, the Inspirational

GUARDIAN

Illus. Kou1

EVOLUTION CREATURE

- 🛡 **Blocker** *(Whenever an opponent's creature attacks, you may tap this creature to stop the attack. Then the 2 creatures battle.)*
- **Evolution—Put on one of your Guardians.**
- **Double breaker** *(This creature breaks 2 shields.)*

9500

©2004 Wizards of the Coast/
Shogakukan/Mitsui-Kids   S1/S5

4 Crystal Paladin

LIQUID PEOPLE

Illus. Eiji Kaneda

EVOLUTION CREATURE

- **Evolution—Put on one of your Liquid People.**
- **When you put this creature into the battle zone, return all creatures in the battle zone that have "blocker" to their owners' hands.**

5000

©2004 Wizards of the Coast/
Shogakukan/Mitsui-Kids   S2/S5

6 Ultracide Worm

PARASITE WORM

Illus. Nakamura Arata

EVOLUTION CREATURE

- **Evolution—Put on one of your Parasite Worms.**
- **Double breaker** *(This creature breaks 2 shields.)*

"Aww. My little Worm is all grown up."
—Ballom, Master of Death

11000

©2004 Wizards of the Coast/
Shogakukan/Mitsui-Kids   S3/S5

4 Armored Blaster Valdios

HUMAN

Illus. Hisashi Momose

EVOLUTION CREATURE

- **Evolution—Put on one of your Humans.**
- **Each of your other Humans in the battle zone gets +1000 power.**
- **Double breaker** *(This creature breaks 2 shields.)*

6000

©2004 Wizards of the Coast/
Shogakukan/Mitsui-Kids   S4/S5

6 Fighter Dual Fang

BEAST FOLK

Illus. Ryoya Yuki

EVOLUTION CREATURE

- **Evolution—Put on one of your Beast Folk.**
- **When you put this creature into the battle zone, put the top 2 cards of your deck into your mana zone.**
- **Double breaker** *(This creature breaks 2 shields.)*

8000

©2004 Wizards of the Coast/
Shogakukan/Mitsui-Kids   S5/S5

Diamond Cutter

5 | SPELL

- This turn, ignore any effects that would prevent your creatures from attacking your opponent. (For example, ignore summoning sickness and card effects that say "This creature can't attack" or "This creature can't attack players." Your creatures can't attack creatures this way.)

©2004 Wizards of the Coast/
Shogakukan/Mitsui-Kids ◆ 1/55

Ethel, Star Sea Elemental

6 | CREATURE
ANGEL COMMAND

- This creature can't be blocked.

The glow of the elementals reaches out even to the stars.

5500 | ©2004 Wizards of the Coast/
Shogakukan/Mitsui-Kids ◎ | 3/55

Fonch, the Oracle

4 | CREATURE
LIGHT BRINGER

- When you put this creature into the battle zone, you may choose one of your opponent's creatures in the battle zone and tap it.

The shining steel oracles choose to stay out of the way and simply observe the invasion . . . for now.

2000 | ©2004 Wizards of the Coast/
Shogakukan/Mitsui-Kids ◆ | 3/55

Laguna, Lightning Enforcer

5 | CREATURE
BERSERKER

- Whenever this creature attacks, search your deck. You may take a spell from your deck, show that spell to your opponent, and put it into your hand. Then shuffle your deck.

The oracles sent the Enforcers to see how badly the cataclysm damaged the planet.

2500 | ©2004 Wizards of the Coast/
Shogakukan/Mitsui-Kids ◆ | 4/55

Larba Geer, the Immaculate

3 | EVOLUTION CREATURE
GUARDIAN

- Evolution—Put on one of your Guardians.
- When you put this creature into the battle zone, tap all your opponent's creatures in the battle zone that have "blocker."

5000 | ©2004 Wizards of the Coast/
Shogakukan/Mitsui-Kids ◆ | 1/55

Logic Cube

3 | SPELL

- Shield trigger (When this spell is put into your hand from your shield zone, you may cast it immediately for no cost.)
- Search your deck. You may take a spell from your deck, show that spell to your opponent, and put it into your hand. Then shuffle your deck.

©2004 Wizards of the Coast/
Shogakukan/Mitsui-Kids ◆ | 6/55

Magris, Vizier of Magnetism

4 | CREATURE
INITIATE

- When you put this creature into the battle zone, you may draw a card.

"Vizier of Magnetism, arise. Your wings a compass that points to the truth." —Hanusa, Radiance Elemental

3000 | ©2004 Wizards of the Coast/
Shogakukan/Mitsui-Kids ◆ | 7/55

Phal Eega, Dawn Guardian

5 | CREATURE
GUARDIAN

- When you put this creature into the battle zone, you may return a spell from your graveyard to your hand.

"Like the sun, I'm just getting warmed up."

4000 | ©2004 Wizards of the Coast/
Shogakukan/Mitsui-Kids ◆ | 3/55

Reso Pacos, Clear Sky Guardian

3 | CREATURE
GUARDIAN

Thanks to their especially keen senses, the Guardians were the first to react to the cataclysm.

3000 | ©2004 Wizards of the Coast/
Shogakukan/Mitsui-Kids ◆ | 9/55

Spiral Grass

4 | CREATURE
STARLIGHT TREE

- Blocker (Whenever an opponent's creature attacks, you may tap this creature to stop the attack. Then the 2 creatures battle.)
- Whenever this creature blocks, untap it after it battles.

2500 | ©2004 Wizards of the Coast/
Shogakukan/Mitsui-Kids ◆ | 10/55

Wyn, the Oracle

2 | CREATURE
LIGHT BRINGER

- Whenever this creature attacks, you may look at one of your opponent's shields. Then put it back where it was.

As the oracles disappeared one by one, they each proclaimed the dawn of a new era.

1500 | ©2004 Wizards of the Coast/
Shogakukan/Mitsui-Kids ◆ | 11/55

LIGHT

Water

Aqua Bouncer
6
LIQUID PEOPLE

CREATURE
- Blocker (Whenever an opponent's creature attacks, you may tap this creature to stop the attack. Then the 2 creatures battle.)
- When you put this creature into the battle zone, you may choose a creature in the battle zone and return it to its owner's hand.

1000

Aqua Shooter
4
LIQUID PEOPLE

CREATURE
- Blocker (Whenever an opponent's creature attacks, you may tap this creature to stop the attack. Then the 2 creatures battle.)

Liquid People can modify their abilities by reprogramming themselves.

2000

Corile
5
CYBER LORD

CREATURE
- When you put this creature into the battle zone, choose one of your opponent's creatures in the battle zone and put it on top of his deck.

When the cataclysm struck, not the science of the Cyber Lords couldn't prevent the collapse of their underwater city.

2000

Crystal Lancer
6
LIQUID PEOPLE

EVOLUTION CREATURE
- Evolution—Put on one of your Liquid People.
- This creature can't be blocked.
- Double breaker (This creature breaks 2 shields.)

8000

Hypersquid Walter
3
CYBER LORD

CREATURE
- Whenever this creature attacks, you may draw a card.

Using the twelve forbidden programs, the Cyber Lords created the elite Liquid People assault troops.

1000

King Nautilus
8
LEVIATHAN

CREATURE
- Liquid People can't be blocked.
- Double breaker (This creature breaks 2 shields.)

Stopping at nothing to their quest for victory, the Cyber Lords transformed even the largest sea creatures into weapons.

6000

Plasma Chaser
6
GEL FISH

CREATURE
- Whenever this creature attacks, you may draw a number of cards equal to the number of creatures your opponent has in the battle zone.

A program to aid the Cyber Lords' land assault, it contains an advanced tracking system designed to function against multiple opponents.

4000

Recon Operation
2

SPELL
- Look at up to 3 of your opponent's shields. Then put them back where they were.

That's not a puddle . . . .

Scissor Eye
4
GEL FISH

CREATURE

The shores of the Fire territory turned blue as wave after wave of Water creatures landed.

3000

Stained Glass
3
CYBER VIRUS

CREATURE
- Whenever this creature attacks, you may choose one of your opponent's fire or nature creatures in the battle zone and return it to its owner's hand.

The only function of Stained Glass, the most adaptable program ever designed by the Cyber Lords, is to help their invasion of the surface world.

1000

Thought Probe
4

SPELL
- Shield trigger (When this spell is put into your hand from your shield zone, you may cast it immediately for no cost.)
- When you cast this spell, if your opponent has 3 or more creatures in the battle zone, draw 3 cards.

Amber Piercer
BRAIN JACKER
4

CREATURE

• Whenever this creature attacks, you may return a creature from your graveyard to your hand.

2000

Amber Piercer
BRAIN JACKER
4

CREATURE

• Whenever this creature attacks, you may return a creature from your graveyard to your hand.

"Let's see what we can dig up."

2000

Dark Titan Maginn
DEMON COMMAND
6

CREATURE

• Whenever this creature attacks, your opponent discards a card at random from his hand.

The forces of Darkness began their invasion by turning the Fiona Woods into a nice, comfortable realm of horror.

4000

Chaos Worm
PARASITE WORM
5

EVOLUTION CREATURE

• Evolution—Put on one of your Parasite Worms.
• When you put this creature into the battle zone, you may destroy one of your opponent's creatures.

5000

Critical Blade
2

SPELL

• Shield trigger *(When this spell is put into your hand from your shield zone, you may cast it immediately for no cost.)*
• Destroy one of your opponent's creatures that has "blocker."

Gray Balloon, Shadow of Greed
GHOST
3

CREATURE

• Blocker *(Whenever an opponent's creature attacks, you may tap this creature to stop the attack. Then the 2 creatures battle.)*
• This creature can't attack players.

It's the thing that goes squish in the night.

3000

General Dark Fiend
DARK LORD
5

CREATURE

• Whenever this creature attacks, choose one of your shields without looking and put it into your graveyard. You can't use the "shield trigger" ability of that shield.
• Double breaker *(This creature breaks 2 shields.)*

6000

Gigastand
CHIMERA
4

CREATURE

• When this creature would be put into your graveyard from the battle zone, you may return it to your hand instead. If you do, discard a card from your hand.

Even nasty, rampaging invaders get a little homesick sometimes.

3000

Marrow Ooze, the Twister
LIVING DEAD
1

CREATURE

• Blocker *(Whenever an opponent's creature attacks, you may tap this creature to stop the attack. Then the 2 creatures battle.)*
• When this creature attacks a player, destroy it after the attack.

1000

Horrid Worm
PARASITE WORM
3

CREATURE

• Whenever this creature attacks, your opponent discards a card at random from his hand.

Worms never refuse a good meal. They never refuse a bad meal either.

2000

Lost Soul
7

SPELL

• Your opponent discards all cards from his hand.

"Looks like you're getting forgetful."

Poison Worm
PARASITE WORM
4

CREATURE

• When you put this creature into the battle zone, destroy one of your creatures that has power 3000 or less.

"You won't get any dessert until you finish eating your friends!"
—Dark Titan Maginn

4000

FIRE

Bombersaur
ROCK BEAST

5

* When this creature is destroyed, each player chooses 2 cards in his mana zone and puts them into his graveyard.

"This species inhabits liquid rock. Highly dangerous."
—Liquid People scouting report

5000

Armored Cannon Balbaro
HUMAN

3

* Evolution—Put one of your Humans.
* While attacking, this creature gets +2000 power for each other Human in the battle zone.

"Can someone reload 'em?"

3000+

Bolzard Dragon
ARMORED DRAGON

6

* Whenever this creature attacks, choose a card in your opponent's mana zone and put it into his graveyard.

When Bolshack awakens in the west, Bolzard roars in the west.

5000

Dogarn, the Marauder
ARMORLOID

3

* While attacking, this creature gets +2000 power for each other tapped creature you have in the battle zone.

With a raucous cry, the first fire reinforcements reached the shore.

2000+

Burst Shot

6

* Shield trigger (When this spell is put into your hand from your shield zone, you may cast it immediately for no cost.)
* Destroy all creatures that have power 2000 or less.

Cavalry General Curatops
DRAGONOID

3

* This creature can attack untapped creatures.

"Doesn't your scooter have a flamethrower, a grenade launcher, a bazooka, and a pair of roto-blades too?"

2000

Metalwing Skyterror
ARMORED WYVERN

7

* Whenever this creature attacks, you may destroy one of your opponent's creatures that has "blocker." (Destroy the creature before your opponent can block with it.)
* Double breaker (This creature breaks 2 shields.)

When fangs and claws aren't pointy enough.

6000

Engineer Kipo
MACHINE EATER

2

* When this creature is destroyed, each player chooses a card in his mana zone and puts it into his graveyard.

"Perfect. Fine. No problem. It's a piece of cake to disassemble these Voltar machines."

2000

Galsaur
ROCK BEAST

5

* While you have no other creatures in the battle zone, this creature has "power attacker +4000" and "double breaker." (A creature that has "power attacker +4000" and "double breaker" gets +4000 power while attacking and breaks 2 shields.)

4000+

Metalwing Skyterror
ARMORED WYVERN

7

* Whenever this creature attacks, you may destroy one of your opponent's creatures that has "blocker." (Destroy the creature before your opponent can block with it.)
* Double breaker (This creature breaks 2 shields.)

6000

Mini Titan Gett
HUMAN

2

* This creature attacks each turn if able.
* Power attacker +1000 (While attacking, this creature gets +1000 power.)

"Someday I'll be strong enough to wear battle armor! You'll see!" —Mini Titan Gett

2000+

Rumble Gate

4

* Each of your creatures in the battle zone gets +1000 power until the end of the turn.
* Each of your creatures in the battle zone that can attack creatures can attack untapped creatures this turn.

It's too soon to let down your guard.

Barkwhip, the Smasher
BEAST FOLK

2

- Evolution—Put on one of your Beast Folk.
- While this creature is tapped, each of your other Beast Folk in the battle zone gets +2000 power.

"Rage leads to war. War leads to rage. Isn't it magical?"
—General Dark Flame

5000

Elf-X
TREE FOLK

4

- Your creatures each cost 1 less to summon. They can't cost less than 1.

The first Chimeras to invade the Flora Woods didn't expect an attack from the forest itself.

2000

Essence Elf
TREE FOLK

2

- Your spells each cost 1 less to cast. They can't cost less than 1.

When the Silver Beards fall, mystical elves come to rescue them.

1000

Fortress Shell
COLONY BEETLE

9

- When you put this creature into the battle zone, choose up to 2 cards in your opponent's mana zone and put them into his graveyard.

"Wow! I can't wait to disassemble this!"
—Named Hero Giant

5000

Leaping Tornado Horn
HORNED BEAST

3

- While attacking, this creature gets +1000 power for each other creature you have in the battle zone.

Beautiful—and deadly—beasts.

2000+

Mana Crisis

4

- **Shield trigger** (When this spell is put into your hand from your shield zone, you may cast it immediately for no cost.)
- Choose a card in your opponent's mana zone and put it into his graveyard.

Rainbow Stone

4

- Search your deck. You may take a card from your deck and put it into your mana zone. Then shuffle your deck.

Pick a color. Any color.

Rumbling Terahorn
HORNED BEAST

5

- When you put this creature into the battle zone, search your deck. You may take a creature from your deck, show that creature to your opponent, and put it into your hand. Then shuffle your deck.

3000

Silver Axe
BEAST FOLK

3

- Whenever this creature attacks, you may put the top card of your deck into your mana zone.

The Silver Beards rose to defend their families and their forest home.

1000

Silver Fist
BEAST FOLK

4

- Power attacker +2000 (While attacking, this creature gets +2000 power.)

"Is one life too high a price to pay to save an entire forest?"

3000+

Xeno Mantis
GIANT INSECT

7

- This creature can't be blocked by any creature that has power 5000 or less.
- Double breaker (This creature breaks 2 shields.)

The invading Worms declared the magical life out of the forest . . . and the cataclysm began.

6000

nature

8 | Miar, Comet Elemental
ANGEL COMMAND

CREATURE

Illus. Jason

- Double breaker *(This creature breaks 2 shields.)*

"Everything on this world exists because we Elementals have given it life."

11500

©2004 Wizards of the Coast/
Shogakukan/Mitsui-Kids ◆ S1/S5

7 | Chaos Fish
GEL FISH

CREATURE

Illus. Akifumi Yamamoto

- This creature gets +1000 power for each other water creature you have in the battle zone.
- Whenever this creature attacks, you may draw a card for each of your other water creatures in the battle zone.

1000+

©2004 Wizards of the Coast/
Shogakukan/Mitsui-Kids ◆ S2/S5

8 | Giriel, Ghastly Warrior
DEMON COMMAND

CREATURE

Illus. Daisuke Izuka

- Double breaker *(This creature breaks 2 shields.)*

Peasant or king, it cares not who its next victim is. It cares only that its victim is warm . . . and very, very scared.

11000

©2004 Wizards of the Coast/
Shogakukan/Mitsui-Kids ◆ S3/S5

7 | Garkago Dragon
ARMORED DRAGON

CREATURE

Illus. Nottsuo

- Double breaker *(This creature breaks 2 shields.)*
- This creature gets +1000 power for each other fire creature you have in the battle zone.
- This creature can attack untapped creatures.

The more you quiver, the more it grows.

6000+

©2004 Wizards of the Coast/
Shogakukan/Mitsui-Kids ◆ S4/S5

5 | Earthstomp Giant
GIANT

CREATURE

Illus. Hiseno Sugiura

- Double breaker *(This creature breaks 2 shields.)*
- Whenever this creature attacks, return all creatures from your mana zone to your hand.

"He's doing real damage to those guys from the opposite Worms! Are you Yomra's or our side?"—Fighter Dual Fang

8000

©2004 Wizards of the Coast/
Shogakukan/Mitsui-Kids ◆ S5/S5

Alek, Solidity Enforcer
BERSERKER

7

CREATURE

Illus. Takeru Kisilo

- **Blocker** *(Whenever an opponent's creature attacks, you may tap this creature to stop the attack. Then the 2 creatures battle.)*
- This creature gets +1000 power for each other light creature you have in the battle zone.

"Hey, you! Get solid!"

4000+

©2004 Wizards of the Coast/
Shogakukan/Mitsui-Kids ★ 1/55

Aless, the Oracle
LIGHT BRINGER

6

CREATURE

Illus. Norikatsu Miyoshi

- When this creature would be put into your graveyard from the battle zone, add it to your shields face down instead.

"Will someone tell Down Giant that I'm not a toy!"

1000

©2004 Wizards of the Coast/
Shogakukan/Mitsui-Kids ★ 2/55

Boomerang Comet

6

SPELL

Illus. Kouichi Kato

- **Shield trigger** *(When this spell is put into your hand from your shield zone, you may cast it immediately for no cost.)*
- Return a card from your mana zone to your hand.
- After you cast this spell, put it into your mana zone instead of your graveyard.

2000

©2004 Wizards of the Coast/
Shogakukan/Mitsui-Kids ★ 3/55

Lena, Vizier of Brilliance
INITIATE

4

CREATURE

Illus. Ryoya Yuki

- When you put this creature into the battle zone, you may return a spell from your mana zone to your hand.

"Vizier of Brilliance, arise. Your fangs are swords of cleansing."
—*Hanusa, Radiance Elemental*

2000

©2004 Wizards of the Coast/
Shogakukan/Mitsui-Kids ★ 4/55

Logic Sphere

3

SPELL

Illus. Daisuke

- **Shield trigger** *(When this spell is put into your hand from your shield zone, you may cast it immediately for no cost.)*
- Return a spell from your mana zone to your hand.

They're all that's holding the planet's atmosphere together.

©2004 Wizards of the Coast/
Shogakukan/Mitsui-Kids ★ 5/55

Ra Vu, Seeker of Lightning
MECHA THUNDER

6

CREATURE

Illus. Toshio Suzuki

- Whenever this creature attacks, you may return a light spell from your graveyard to your hand.

"I am the eye of the hurricane of endless destruction."

4000

©2004 Wizards of the Coast/
Shogakukan/Mitsui-Kids ★ 6/55

Raza Vega, Thunder Guardian
GUARDIAN

10

CREATURE

Illus. Akira Hamada

- **Blocker** *(Whenever an opponent's creature attacks, you may tap this creature to stop the attack. Then the 2 creatures battle.)*
- When this creature would be put into your graveyard from the battle zone, add it to your shields face down instead.

3000

©2004 Wizards of the Coast/
Shogakukan/Mitsui-Kids ★ 7/55

Sieg Balicula, the Intense
INITIATE

3

EVOLUTION CREATURE

Illus. Masaki Hirooka

- Evolution—Put on one of your Initiates.
- Each of your other light creatures in the battle zone has "blocker." *(Whenever one of your opponent's creatures attacks, you may tap a creature that has "blocker" to stop the attack. Then the 2 creatures battle.)*

5000

©2004 Wizards of the Coast/
Shogakukan/Mitsui-Kids ★ 8/55

Sparkle Flower
STARLIGHT TREE

4

CREATURE

Illus. Hayashi Morosse

- While all the cards in your mana zone are light cards, this creature has "Blocker" *(Whenever an opponent's creature attacks, you may tap this creature to stop the attack. Then the 2 creatures battle.)*

From tiny seeds grow giant, tree-like, spiral-matrix shingles.

3000

©2004 Wizards of the Coast/
Shogakukan/Mitsui-Kids ★ 9/55

Sundrop Armor

4

SPELL

Illus. Sontyo

- Add a card from your hand to your shields face down.

"The danger hasn't passed. But we have."
—*Mitar, Comet Elemental*

©2004 Wizards of the Coast/
Shogakukan/Mitsui-Kids ★ 10/55

Ur Pale, Seeker of Sunlight
MECHA THUNDER

4

CREATURE

Illus. Naoki Saito

- While all the cards in your mana zone are light cards, this creature gets +2000 power.

"What will it do if it finds the sunlight?" —*Bloody Squito*

2500+

©2004 Wizards of the Coast/
Shogakukan/Mitsui-Kids ★ 11/55

LIGHT

water

Angler Cluster
3
CYBER CLUSTER

- Blocker (Whenever an opponent's creature attacks, you may tap this creature to stop the attack. Then the 2 creatures battle.)
- This creature can't attack.
- While all the cards in your hand are water cards, this creature gets +3000 power.

3000+

Aqua Deformer
8
LIQUID PEOPLE

- When you put this creature into the battle zone, return 2 cards from your mana zone to your hand. Then your opponent chooses 2 cards in his mana zone and returns them to his hand.

Nothing is quite what it seems.

3000

Emeral
2
CYBER LORD

- When you put this creature into the battle zone, you may add a card from your hand to your shields face down. If you do, choose one of your shields and put it into your hand. You can't use the "shield trigger" ability of that shield.

"If you think I'm good at this, watch me play video games."

1000

Flood Valve
2

- Shield trigger (When this spell is put into your hand from your shield zone, you may cast it immediately for no cost.)
- Return a card from your mana zone to your hand.

"Open up freshwater valve 23D. I'm thirsty."

King Neptas
6
LEVIATHAN

- Whenever this creature attacks, you may choose a creature in the battle zone that has power 2000 or less and return it to its owner's hand. (Return the creature to its owner's hand before your opponent can block with it.)

A swarm of fish surround it, hoping to feed on its leftovers.

5000

King Ponitas
8
LEVIATHAN

- Whenever this creature attacks, search your deck. You may take a water card from your deck, show that card to your opponent, and put it into your hand. Then shuffle your deck.

"I caught five fishermen today. But you should have seen the one that got away!"

4000

Legendary Bynor
6
LEVIATHAN

EVOLUTION CREATURE
- Evolution—Put on one of your Leviathans.
- Your other water creatures in the battle zone can't be blocked.
- Double breaker (This creature breaks 2 shields.)

"I can see my ocean from here."

8000

Liquid Scope
4

- Shield trigger (When this spell is put into your hand from your shield zone, you may cast it immediately for no cost.)
- Look at your opponent's hand and shields. Then put the shields back where they were.

"Let's find out if your brain is ticklish." —Legendary Bynor

Psychic Shaper
6

- Reveal the top 4 cards of your deck. Put all water cards from among them into your hand and the rest into your graveyard.

Think. Think harder. No, not that hard.

Shtra
4
CYBER LORD

- When you put this creature into the battle zone, return a card from your mana zone to your hand. Then your opponent chooses a card in his mana zone and returns it to his hand.

Living underwater means never having to take a bath.

2000

Stinger Ball
3
CYBER VIRUS

- Whenever this creature attacks, you may look at one of your opponent's shields. Then put it back where it was.

The eyes have it.

1000

50

Baraga, Blade of Gloom
DARK LORD

4

CREATURE

- When you put this creature into the battle zone, choose one of your shields and put it into your hand. You can't use the "shield trigger" ability of that shield.

"War isn't a game. Sure, one side wins, the other side loses, and it's a lot of fun, but . . . well. . . hey, maybe it is a game."

4000

Bone Piercer
BRAIN JACKER

2

CREATURE

- When this creature is put into your graveyard from the battle zone, you may return a creature from your mana zone to your hand.

"What do you mean that's not food? Just give me some ketchup!"

1000

Eldritch Poison

1

SPELL

- ◆ Shield trigger (When this spell is put into your hand from your shield zone, you may cast it immediately for no cost.)
- You may destroy one of your darkness creatures. If you do, return a creature from your mana zone to your hand.

Gamil, Knight of Hatred
DEMON COMMAND

6

CREATURE

- Whenever this creature attacks, you may return a darkness creature from your graveyard to your hand.

The holes it digs its friends out of are the holes it buries its enemies in.

4000

Ghastly Drain

3

SPELL

- Choose any number of your shields and put them into your hand. You can't use the "shield trigger" abilities of those shields.

If you're not getting nightmares, you're not trying hard enough.

Hang Worm, Fetid Larva
PARASITE WORM

5

CREATURE

From the rotting trees of the Fiona Woods, a new horror oozes forth.

4000

Jack Viper, Shadow of Doom
GHOST

3

EVOLUTION CREATURE

- Evolution—Put on one of your Ghosts.
- Whenever another of your darkness creatures would be put into your graveyard from the battle zone, you may return it to your hand instead.

Has it conquered death, or has it just replaced it with something worse?

4000

Mudman
HEDRIAN

4

CREATURE

- While all the cards in your mana zone are darkness cards, this creature gets +2000 power.

"We all crawl from the slime. Someday, we'll all return to it."

2000+

Scratchclaw
HEDRIAN

4

CREATURE

- Slayer (When this creature loses a battle, destroy the other creature.)
- This creature gets +1000 power for each other darkness creature you have in the battle zone.

"Uh oh. My nose itches."

1000+

Snake Attack

4

SPELL

- Each of your creatures in the battle zone gets "double breaker" until the end of the turn. (A creature that has "double breaker" breaks 2 shields.)
- Choose one of your shields and put it into your graveyard.

Baraga unsuccessfully gave swords to his army of snakes.

Wailing Shadow Belbetphlo
GHOST

3

CREATURE

- Slayer (When this creature loses a battle, destroy the other creature.)

The faster it runs from its pain, the faster its pain catches others.

1000

DARKNESS

FIRE

5 | Armored Warrior Quelos
ARMORLOID

- Whenever this creature attacks, put a non-fire card from your mana zone into your graveyard. Then your opponent chooses a non-fire card in his mana zone and puts it into his graveyard.

When you can create creatures at will, you don't have to aim too carefully.

2000

3 | Baby Zoppe
FIRE BIRD

- While all the cards in your mana zone are fire cards, this creature gets +2000 power.

Some Fire Birds are so eager to get into battle they don't bother to finish hatching first.

2000+

7 | Blaze Cannon

- You can cast this spell only if all the cards in your mana zone are fire cards.
- Each of your creatures in the battle zone gets "power attacker +4000" and "double breaker" until the end of the turn. (A creature that has "power attacker +4000" and "double breaker" gets +4000 power while attacking and breaks 2 shields.)

9000

7 | Boltail Dragon
ARMORED DRAGON

- Double breaker (This creature breaks 2 shields.)

"Leviathans? I can juggle Leviathans!"

9000

3 | Explosive Dude Joe
HUMAN

"I used to have a real problem with exploding. But now, thanks to a balanced diet and regular exercise, I've cut my explosion rate to twice a day. I can't take all the credit, though. The support of my wonderful family has finally let me lead a normal"—BOOM!

3000

4 | Flametropus
ROCK BEAST

- Whenever this creature attacks, you may put a card from your mana zone into your graveyard. If you do, this creature gets "power attacker +3000" and "double breaker" until the end of the turn. (A creature that has "power attacker +3000" and "double breaker" gets +3000 power while attacking and breaks 2 shields.)

3000+

6 | Muramasa, Duke of Blades
HUMAN

- Whenever this creature attacks, you may destroy one of your opponent's creatures that has power 2000 or less.

"If I can't teach you respect, my Ultimate Astral Strike will!"

3000

5 | Searing Wave

- Destroy all your opponent's creatures that have power 3000 or less.
- Choose one of your shields and put it into your graveyard.

Surf's up!

2 | Snip Striker Bullraizer
DRAGONOID

- This creature can't attack while your opponent has more creatures in the battle zone than you do.

"You're getting more than just a haircut."

3000

7 | Überdragon Jabaha
ARMORED DRAGON

- Evolution—Put on one of your Armored Dragons.
- Each of your other fire creatures in the battle zone has "power attacker +2000." (While attacking, a creature that has "power attacker +2000" gets +2000 power.)
- Double breaker (This creature breaks 2 shields.)

11000

2 | Volcanic Arrows

- Shield trigger (When this spell is put into your hand from your shield zone, you may cast it immediately for no cost.)
- Destroy a creature that has power 6000 or less.
- Choose one of your shields and put it into your graveyard.

Aurora of Reversal

5

SPELL

- Choose any number of your shields and put them into your mana zone.

The forest hasn't grown this fast since the ancient invasion of the fertilizer fiends.

Dawn Giant

7

GIANT

CREATURE

- This creature can't attack creatures.
- Double breaker (This creature breaks 2 shields.)

That's not the sound of an earthquake. That's just the Dawn Giants snoring.

11000

Gigamantis

4

GIANT INSECT

EVOLUTION CREATURE

- Evolution—Put on one of your Giant Insects.
- Whenever another of your nature creatures would be put into your graveyard from the battle zone, put it into your mana zone instead.

"But I don't wanna be a tree!" —Four Fang

5000

Mana Nexus

4

SPELL

- Shield trigger (When this spell is put into your shield zone from your hand, you may cast it immediately for no cost.)
- Add a card from your mana zone to your shields face down.

Masked Pomegranate

5

TREE FOLK

CREATURE

- This creature gets +1000 power for each of your other nature creatures in the battle zone.
- This creature can't be blocked by any creature that has power 4000 or less.

It's related to the raspberry bush.

1000+

Pouch Shell

4

COLONY BEETLE

CREATURE

- When you put this creature into the battle zone, you may choose one of your opponent's evolution creatures in the battle zone and put the top card of that creature into your opponent's graveyard.

A blast to the past.

1000

Psyshroom

4

BALLOON MUSHROOM

CREATURE

- Whenever this creature attacks, you may put a nature card from your graveyard into your mana zone.

Young Balloon Mushrooms think pizzas exist only in horror stories their parents use to scare them. When they grow up, they learn the awful truth.

2000

Raging Dash-Horn

5

HORNED BEAST

CREATURE

- While all the cards in your mana zone are nature cards, this creature gets +3000 power and has "Double breaker (This creature breaks 2 shields)."

The night the Flame Wands were finally defeated, the sky echoed their cries of rage.

4000+

Roar of the Earth

2

SPELL

- Shield trigger (When this spell is put into your hand from your shield zone, you may cast it immediately for no cost.)
- Return a creature that costs 6 or more from your mana zone to your hand.

When danger looms, heroes rise.

Sniper Mosquito

1

GIANT INSECT

CREATURE

- Whenever this creature attacks, return a card from your mana zone to your hand.

It prefers drinking tree sap over drinking blood. But everything else needs a distant third.

2000

Sword Butterfly

3

GIANT INSECT

CREATURE

- Power attacker +3000 (While attacking, this creature gets +3000 power.)

One mouthful of its pollen can knock out a Horned Beast for a week.

2000+

nature

FIRE/DARKNESS
SPEED

Creatures (26)

4 Deadly Fighter Braid Claw

4 Marrow Ooze, the Twister

4 Mini Titan Gett

4 Engineer Kipo

2 Writhing Bone Ghoul

4 Horrid Worm

4 Rothus, the Traveler

Spells (14)

4 Crimson Hammer

4 Critical Blade

2 Magma Gazer

4 Death Smoke

Mana Ceiling: Four mana for **Rothus, the Traveler** and **Death Smoke.**

Average Mana Cost: 2.4

Plan

This is one of the fastest decks. It has eight creatures that only cost one mana and ten more that only cost two. There are twelve spells that remove opposing creatures at varying mana costs, and eight of those will destroy a Blocker for four mana or less.

Simply cast creatures and then attack with them when the summoning sickness wears off. Careful with **Marrow Ooze, the Twister**, though. He dies after attacking once, so don't use him until your big push to destroy your opponent.

If your opponent stops your early attackers, don't give up hope. Against decks without Blockers, break four or five shields, then wait a few turns and summon multiple small creatures.

Light and Water decks with cheap Blockers are your biggest threat — their creatures are larger and not more expensive. Your best chance is to draw **Critical Blades** and **Death Smokes** to destroy the Blockers.

Card Choices

Mini Titan Gett is one of the best two mana creatures because he has 2000 power and Power Attacker.

Engineer Kipo causes both players to lose a card from their mana zone when he goes to the graveyard, which seems bad, but hurts decks with more expensive creatures more than it does yours. The one-turn delay can often make the difference between you winning and your opponent casting something to stop you. If your opponent chooses not to destroy **Kipo**, he'll keep on attacking.

Horrid Worm forces your opponent to discard a card when he attacks. The card is discarded at random, so you might take out something crucial.

When you summon **Rothus, the Traveler,** both players lose a creature from the battle zone. Even if **Rothus** dies from his own ability, he still destroyed an enemy creature, and sometimes you'll want to sacrifice something else to keep him around. Remember that he'll have summoning sickness and the sacrificed creature probably didn't, though.

Use **Death Smoke**, a spell which destroys an untapped creature, to destroy a large creature that's just been summoned. It can take out Blockers, too!

Crimson Hammer is your cheapest option for destroying enemy creatures. Put it in the mana zone if the other deck doesn't have small creatures.

Magma Gazer lets a creature break two shields at once. Cast it before you start attacking, but wait until you know you can break a shield. If you attack with other creatures first you risk losing your pumped up creature to a Shield Trigger.

Potential Improvements

The most unpredictable card is probably **Magma Gazer**, so start changes there. **Amber Piercer**, a Darkness creature that returns a creature from your graveyard each time it attacks, can give your deck more staying power. Another option is **Artisan Picora**, a one-mana Fire creature with the drawback of removing a card from your mana zone.

Whenever a new set comes out, take a look at all the Fire and Darkness creatures that cost four or less and try them out for a few games. Check out the cheap spells, too. Can any of them destroy creatures or Blockers for less mana than your current spells?

FIRE/NATURE
BEAST FOLK

Creatures (29)

- 4 Burning Mane
- 4 Barkwhip, the Smasher
- 4 Bronze-Arm Tribe
- 3 Fear Fang
- 3 Mighty Shouter
- 4 Rumbling Terahorn
- 2 Explosive Fighter Ucarn
- 3 Bolshack Dragon
- 2 Fighter Dual Fang

Spells (11)

- 4 Tornado Flame
- 3 Burst Shot
- 4 Natural Snare

Mana Ceiling: Nothing in the deck costs more than six, but you'll often have more than that in your mana zone due to the **Bronze-Arm Tribes, Mighty Shouters**, and **Fighter Dual Fangs**.

Average Mana Cost: 4.2

Plan

The Evo-Crushinators of Doom creatures require building your deck around them. Get **Barkwhip, the Smasher** into play early. He makes your other Beast Folk the largest creatures in the battle zone. If your opponent manages to survive their assault, you've got extra surprises: **Fighter Dual Fang, Bolshack Dragon**, and **Explosive Fighter Ucarn**. These all break two shields.

If your opponent is destroying all your creatures, remember that Evolution creatures can attack on their first turn. Play a **Burning Mane** and an Evolution card and immediately attack! When your opponent is low on shields, he's never safe. Or cast a **Rumbling Terahorn**. When searching your deck for a creature, find *another* **Terahorn**

. . . until all four **Terahorns** are out. Then you'll have a stream of creatures to face your opponent. When you summon the last **Terahorn**, search out a **Bolshack Dragon** or **Fighter Dual Fang** to really put the pressure on.

Card Choices

The cheap Beast Folk make it easier to evolve your **Barkwhips** and **Fighter Dual Fangs**.

The spells are all Shield Triggers so you'll have lots of surprises for your opponent.

Against decks with cheap creatures, the three **Burst Shots** destroy their whole army. **Explosive Fighter Ucarn** requires you to put two cards from your mana zone into your graveyard, but that's not a problem. Between the **Bronze-Arm Tribes** and the **Fighter Dual Fangs**, you have plenty of extra cards. Once you make the sacrifice, you have a 9000 power creature for only five mana!

Rumbling Terahorn gives you more staying power against decks that destroy your creatures slowly. Late in the game, it also finds the perfect creature to win.

Potential Improvements

As **Fighter Dual Fang** is a super rare, it might be hard to find two copies. Until you get them, **Xeno Mantis** or **Roaring Great Horn** are good replacements. If you have more than two **Fighter Dual Fangs**, though, don't hesitate to add all of them. A creature with 8000 power that puts two free cards into your mana zone is an amazing combination!

Another great super rare is **Scarlet Skyterror**. This eight-mana Fire creature destroys all Blockers. It single-handedly defeats most Light-based decks. Search for it with a **Rumbling Terahorn**.

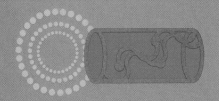

LIGHT/WATER

CONTROL

Creatures (28)

4 Emerald Grass

2 Aqua Vehicle

4 Senatine Jade Tree

4 Aqua Hulcus

4 Dia Nork, Moonlight Guardian

2 Aqua Knight

4 Gran Gure, Space Guardian

4 Crystal Lancer

Spells (12)

4 Thought Probe

4 Holy Awe

4 Terror Pit

Mana Ceiling: Six for **Holy Awe**, **Terror Pit**, and **Crystal Lancer**. But if your opponent is destroying your Liquid People, go to eight to summon an **Aqua Vehicle** and evolve it into a **Crystal Paladin** in the same turn.

Average Mana Cost: 4.35

Plan

This deck stops your opponent's threats with Blockers from the Light civilization. These Blockers can attack tapped creatures, and **Holy Awe** taps all your opponent's creatures, so you can destroy them.

Thought Probe and **Aqua Hulcus** let you draw cards, so you'll have extra. With that advantage, you want the duel to run long.

The four **Terror Pits** give your shields flexibility and can be cast to remove troublesome creatures later. They're the only Darkness cards, so place the first **Terror Pit** you draw into the mana zone.

Once you're feeling safe, start attacking. Because the four **Crystal Lancers** can't be blocked and break two shields in one attack, you can win with nothing but them even if they're attacked or destroyed with Shield Triggers.

Remember to save up Liquid People so you'll have something to evolve.

Card Choices

The deck uses all Light Blockers since Water Blockers can't attack.

Aqua Knight is included to defy decks that destroy all creatures instantly. It's a fairly big creature, and it returns to your hand each time it dies, so those decks will have trouble unless they send it to your mana zone instead. It's also a Liquid Person for evolution purposes.

Thought Probe only works when your opponent has three or more creatures in the battle zone . . . but that's what happens when you're using Blockers. It's also a Shield Trigger, which is a nice bonus.

LIGHT/WATER CONTROL

The **Terror Pits** allow you to deal with large Evolution creatures. If you don't have a **Gran Gure, Space Guardian**, anything over 5000 power is a problem. In most games, you won't be able to cast a **Terror Pit**, but one in your shields could turn losses into wins.

Possible Improvements

With all the Blockers, you shouldn't have trouble with fast decks . . . but if you do, include **La Ura Giga, Sky Guardian**. A one-mana Blocker will nullify your opponent's fastest draws.

King Depthcon, a super rare, is another winning option. It has 6000 power, is a Double Breaker, and can't be blocked, yet it costs only seven mana. It can't attack on its first turn, but unlike **Crystal Paladin**, you don't have to evolve a Liquid Person to use it.

Scarlet Skyterror might a problem, since it destroys all Blockers. Add a few **Lost Souls**, which make your opponent discard his entire hand and might help knock **Scarlet** out. Also hold backup Blockers in your hand.

FIRE/NATURE/DARKNESS

DESTROY 'EM ALL

Creatures (24)

4 Rothus the Traveler

4 Bloody Squito

4 Bronze-Arm Tribe

2 Gigargon

4 Storm Shell

4 Swamp Worm

2 Meteosaur

Spells (16)

4 Death Smoke

4 Tornado Flame

4 Terror Pit

4 Natural Snare

Mana Ceiling: Go straight to seven mana for your **Swamp Worms** and **Storm Shells**, but you may need to go up to eight for **Gigargon**.

Average Mana Cost: 5.05

Plan

The cards in this deck cost more mana, on average, than any other deck in this guide — because you're not out to destroy your opponent right away. You want to send his creatures to the graveyard one by one. Thirty of the forty cards destroy an opposing creature.

In the first five or six turns of the game, trade one card of yours for one of your opponent's. Your **Bloody Squito** blocks an attacker and both die. Your **Death Smoke** destroys a creature he just summoned. He breaks one of your shields and your **Terror Pit** destroys a potential attacker. Your only goal is to stay alive.

Late in the game, start playing **Meteosaur** and **Swamp Worm**, which destroy creatures and also stay in the battle zone. Remember not to attack too soon, because each shield you break might be another creature to destroy, and you're probably low on shields. Once you have three or four more creatures than your opponent, attack shields to put him out of his misery.

Card Choices

Four different cards are in the deck to help you stay alive early on. **Terror Pit**, **Tornado Flame**, and **Natural Trap** are all Shield Triggers. Always have at least one Shield Trigger waiting to surprise your opponent.

Bloody Squito, a 4000 power Blocker for only two mana, also helps against quick creature strategies.

Bronze-Arm Tribe lets you put the top card of your deck into your mana zone. That helps get cards from all three civilizations into your mana zone, and racks up five mana by turn four so you can cast your powerful spells earlier.

Gigargon returns two creatures from your graveyard to your hand. Having two of these ensures a steady stream of **Swamp Worms** and **Storm Shells**.

Remember, you can cast **Rothus, the Traveler** even if you don't have other creatures in play. He provides a cheap way to send an opponent's creature to the graveyard. Sometimes, though, choose a **Bronze-Arm Tribe** or **Gigargon** that's already done its job to sacrifice instead, and keep the 4000 power **Rothus** in the battle zone.

Possible Improvements

This deck already is set up to accomplish its single-minded goal, but there are some possible changes. One tempting card is **Chaos Worm** from Evo-Crushinators of Doom. It lets you choose an opponent's creature to send to the graveyard. One problem: It needs to evolve from another Parasite Worm. If you add **Chaos Worms** to your deck, also add four **Horrid Worms.**

If you're losing to speedy decks, include up to four **Burst Shots**. **Burst Shot** is a six-mana Fire spell that destroys all creatures with 2000 power or less. It's also a Shield Trigger, so you can wipe out quick creatures in the early turns.

If you're up against a deck using cards like **Brain Serum**, add a few **Lost Souls**. These will punish any deck trying to draw more cards than one per turn.

FIRE/WATER

TEMPO

Creatures (32)

4 Deadly Fighter Braid Claw

4 Mini Titan Gett

4 Immortal Baron, Vorg

4 Engineer Kipo

4 Aqua Hulcus

2 Stained Glass

4 Unicorn Fish

4 Corile

2 Meteosaur

Spells (8)

4 Spiral Gate

4 Teleportation

Mana Ceiling: Go to five mana for **Corile, Meteosaur,** and **Teleportation**, and then stop putting cards in the mana zone.

Average Mana Cost: 3.00

Plan

This deck puts the pressure on immediately and then never lets up. In the early turns, cast your cheap creatures to hit your opponent's shields as your expensive spells clear the way. Whenever your opponent puts a creature in the battle zone, make sure it's not there by the end of your turn. You have twelve creatures and eight spells that can accomplish this.

Along with the broken shields, your opponent will be gaining a full hand from creatures returning from your **Spiral Gates.** Finish him off before those cards matter. Keep attacking, casting creatures, and clearing the way with **Teleportations** and **Coriles** until you hit for the final blow.

Card Choices

Fire has better offensive creatures than Water does, so all of the early attackers are from that civilization. **Deadly Fighter Braid Claw**, **Mini Titan Gett**, **Immortal Baron**, and **Engineer Kipo** all cost only one or two mana.

At three mana, you have **Aqua Hulcus**, which draws a card when it comes into play.

You also have two copies of **Stained Glass**, a devastating creature against Fire and Nature decks. Against other civilizations put it into the mana zone early.

At the four and five mana mark, you have **Unicorn Fish** and **Corile**, two creatures that remove an opposing creature from the battle zone.

There's no real need to include Shield Triggers — if you start losing shields while playing this deck, you're in trouble. Focus on putting pressure on your opponent instead. However, **Spiral Gate** is a Shield Trigger that lets you bounce a creature back to your opponent's hand for only two mana.

Teleportation is a way to win games out of nowhere by removing two creatures at once. Early in the game, put it in the mana zone, but if you draw it later, you'll be very happy it's in your deck.

Possible Improvements

Add a third and fourth **Stained Glass** to play against a deck with Fire or Nature creatures. This method of returning creatures to your opponent's hand is very powerful.

If you play against Water decks with Blockers, **Candy Drop** is a good option. It's a cheap creature that can't be blocked. It's not as strong against Light blockers, since it only has 1000 power. Even then, though, **Candy Drop** can break a shield before dying.

Add **Crimson Hammers** if you're playing against a deck with small creatures.

Building a new deck from scratch can be a little overwhelming, but there's no better feeling than winning duels with forty cards that you chose.

Have a Plan

The decks in the previous section each have a plan for winning. For some it's winning as fast as possible, for some it's destroying everything the opponent plays, and for some it's blocking until you have total control of the battle zone. Without a plan, you'll just end up selecting forty of your favorite cards and shuffling them. While that's fun, it's not the best way to build a strong deck.

So . . . come up with a plan.
• How does your deck plan on winning?
• Is it going to concentrate on winning in the first few turns?
• Is it going to just try to survive so that it can win in the late game?
• Does it plan on dealing with enemy creatures using Blockers, spells, or Shield Triggers?

How Many Civilizations?

Ask yourself what civilizations you want to include. The more civilizations you put in your deck, the more likely it is that you won't be able to cast spells or creatures in your hand. Since you have to put at least one card from each civilization in your mana zone, you'll never be able to summon a creature if it's the only card from that civilization that you've drawn. Even if you have two cards from a civilization, you'll still only be able to cast one of them.

Most decks use two or three civilizations, because there isn't a good reason to stick to one. Each civilization has its strengths and weaknesses, so it makes sense to diversify.

Mana Curve

After planning your strategy, arrange your cards in order of how much mana they cost to play. Choose cards that have different mana costs.

If everything costs six or more, you won't be able to summon creatures until it's too late.

Or, if all forty cards cost three mana, on turns four and five you'll be wasting mana because you'll still be summoning three-mana creatures while your opponent has moved on to bigger things.

Speed decks have a lot of cheap creatures since they don't expect the game to last long, but even then vary the costs so that you use all your mana each turn.

Mana Ceiling

Remember, the lower you keep your mana ceiling, the more spell and creature cards you'll have available. Each card you don't put in your mana zone is another card that you can use to win.

Don't avoid adding Bolshack Dragon to your deck just because it costs six mana, but if you're playing a fast deck and nothing else in your deck costs more than four, it's probably not worth raising your mana ceiling that far.

Shield Triggers

Think about the number of spells with Shield Trigger in your deck. Shield Triggers are a great way for slower decks to survive against fast decks because you can cast expensive spells much earlier. If you're playing a deck that will likely lose most of its shields, it makes sense to have eight to twelve copies of spells with Shield Trigger. Look at the Destroy 'Em All deck (Page 64) as an example. On the other hand, a faster deck like Fire/Darkness Speed (Page 54) hardly has any Shield Triggers at all.

Evolution Creatures

Think about including some Evolution creatures. Not only are they extremely powerful, but they can also attack the turn they come into play. Make sure that you have enough creatures of the proper race to support it. Usually you'll want around eight, although if you have more copies of the Evolution creature you might want even more. Look at the Fire/Nature Beast Folk deck (Page 57) for an example of an Evolution-based deck. Notice the fourteen non-Evolution Beast Folk in it.

Putting It All Together

Gather an assortment of forty cards. While there's no rule that says you can't have more than forty, you should keep your deck exactly at forty so that it can carry out your plan as efficiently as possible.

Then head down to the local game store and challenge some people to duels. After five or ten duels, you should have a better feel for what's working, so keep adjusting your deck until it's as perfect as it can be.

You'll be winning tournaments in no time!

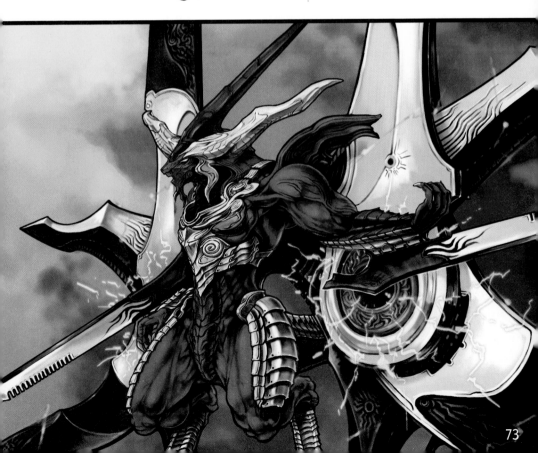

TRADING AND COLLECTING CARDS

There are three ways to build your collection: trading with other players, buying booster packs, and buying single cards. When you're just starting out and you don't have much of a collection yet, buying booster packs is definitely the way to go. Once you have a good base of cards, it's time to start looking for specific cards, either for the purposes of completing a collection or for putting them into decks.

There are five different levels of rarity:

Rarity Chart

✚ super rare

✪ very rare

★ rare

✦ uncommon

● common

You can recognize very rares and super rares because the holographic treatment. On super rares, the art bursts out of the frame!

Finishing a Collection

If you want to complete a collection, your goal is to acquire at least one of every card from a certain set. Don't worry about the power level of the cards that you're getting.

The card collector numbers in the bottom right are there to help you see what you have and how far you have to go. Fatal Attacker Horvath from the Base Set, for example, is labeled with 77/110. This means that there are 110 cards in the Base Set, and that one is number 77. The super rares have their own special numbers from S1 to S10, so you can finish a collection with just the commons through very rares. For a full collection, though, you should try to get the super rares, too.

TRADING AND COLLECTING CARDS

Finding Cards For Decks

Perhaps you want to put a certain card into your deck but you simply haven't received it in your booster packs. Or maybe you're fighting a duel and someone beats you with a brand new card that you've never seen before. When you need specific cards, trade with other Duel Masters players.

Trading

Check at your local game store to get a feel for the value of certain cards. Ask for the prices on certain cards, or just browse if they have them in a display case. Take note of the cards that are worth a lot more than the other ones, because you should be able to get more cards if you offer them for trade.

Also watch other people duel and pay attention to the cards they use. If a card is in a lot of different decks, it's definitely more valuable than the other equally-rare cards. Cards like Terror Pit and Bronze-Arm Tribe are good examples of this, whereas a card like Laser Wing probably won't be in too many decks since Holy Awe has a much better effect (and is a Shield Trigger) for only one more mana.

Until you get a lot of experience with trading, make sure that the cards you're giving away and the cards you're getting have close to the same value according to the store. If you can't find prices, though, you can always fall back on the rarity. If you trade uncommons for uncommons, rares for rares, and so on, you'll almost always be getting a fair deal. Remember to check the rarity symbol in the bottom right.

preparing for a tournament

After you've been playing Duel Masters for a few months, you might hear about tournaments taking place. The idea of playing in a tournament with a lot of other people can be scary at first, but it's actually not that different than dueling with your friends.

And you can win prizes if you do well!

Choosing Your Deck
Since you'll be using the same deck for the entire tournament, think carefully about which you should use. Pay attention to the decks that other people seem to own and use, so that you can try to pick a deck that matches up against them. If you see that a lot of players are running fast decks, look at playing a deck with a lot of Blockers and Shield Triggers. If people are playing decks with a lot of big creatures and expensive spells, run a fast deck yourself.

Always go with a deck that makes you feel comfortable. Don't make the mistake of playing something that you built the night before. Practice duels are important because they teach you how to play the deck.

Sleep and Food
It may be tempting to stay up late the night before, testing your deck with your friends, but it's important that you get enough sleep. Tournaments can take anywhere from four to ten hours, so you're going to be doing a lot of thinking. Without sleep, you'll make mistakes and lose duels that you should have won. It's also important to make sure that you eat a good breakfast and find time to get lunch.

Get There Early
It's a good idea to leave some extra time in the morning. Maybe you'll get lost on the way to the tournament site, or maybe you want to add a card to your deck because it'd be good against the decks that other people seem to have. You never

know what might happen and nothing's more disappointing than arriving at the site and finding they've started without you.

The Actual Tournament

Don't worry if you're a little nervous when the tournament is starting. Eventually the Tournament Organizer will announce that pairings have been posted, at which point you need to find your name on a sheet of paper that tells you where to sit. When your first opponent sits down across from you, it's time to duel. Have confidence in your deck and your skill as a player and you should do fine. Good luck!

Every three months, a new set of cards is released that expands the Duel Masters universe. Each set contains exciting new creatures and powerful spells for each of the five civilizations. Even when you think you've made the best deck possible, you'll be able to keep improving it because new cards are constantly added.

While the new cards won't necessarily be more powerful than your current cards, they'll have different effects and give you more flexibility when building your deck. Sometimes you'll even find a card that inspires you to build a completely new deck or try out a new civilization.

Even if none of the other reasons existed, remember: When building a deck full of giant monsters, you can never have too many options!

Upcoming Sets

Shadowclash of Blinding Night
Survivors of the Megapocalypse